MANO ANDOY'S SIGNS

D1204552

NOT TO BE WRITTEN ON • PROPERTY OF THE PUBLIC LIBRARY • OFFICE

STORY BY
MAILIN PATERNO

PICTURES BY
ISABEL ROXAS

FILIPINO TRANSLATION BY
EUGENE Y. EVASCO

TAHANAN BOOKS FOR YOUNG READERS
MANILA

For Bee and Teo
M.P.L.

For the unheralded sign painters and vinyl cutters
of the Philippine Islands, as well as my fellow typophiles
and lovers of vernacular design
I.R.

Published by Tahanan Books for Young Readers
A division of Ilaw ng Tahanan Publishing, Inc.
Unit 402, Cityland III Condominium
105 V.A. Rufino corner Esteban Street
Legaspi Village, Makati City, 1229 Philippines
Sales and marketing telefax: (63-2) 813-7165
Email: marketing@tahananbooks.com

www.tahananbooks.com

Text copyright © 2015 by Maria Elena Paterno and Ilaw ng Tahanan Publishing, Inc.
Illustrations copyright © 2015 by Isabel Roxas and Ilaw ng Tahanan Publishing, Inc.
All rights reserved.
This book may not be reproduced, in whole or in part, in any form,
without written permission from the publisher.

Filipino translator: Eugene Y. Evasco

Printed in the Philippines by Print Town
10   9   8   7   6   5   4   3   2   1
First Edition

The National Library of the Philippines Cataloging-in-Publication Data

Recommended entry:

Paterno, Maria Elena.
    Mang Andoy's signs / written by Mailin Paterno ;
pictures by Isabel Roxas. Makati City : Tahanan Books
for Young Readers, [c2015].

    p. ; cm.

    In Filipino and English text.
    ISBN 978-971-630-182-3

    1. Readers (Elementary) 2. Street signs—Juvenile literature.
3. Signs and symbols—Juvenile literature. I. Roxas, Isabel. II. Title.

372.40834 LB1573 2015 P420140182

The artwork for this book was created using watercolor, paper scraps,
and digital collage. Bus fare tickets, candy wrappers, and other pieces of vintage
ephemera were collected from bus conductors, friends, and generous pack rats.

Mang Andoy was a quiet man
who made signs.

Tahimik na tao si Mang Andoy
na gumagawa ng mga karatula.

He kept a tidy workshop in the
middle of a crowded, noisy city.

*May maayos siyang pagawaan sa gitna
ng masikip at magulong siyudad.*

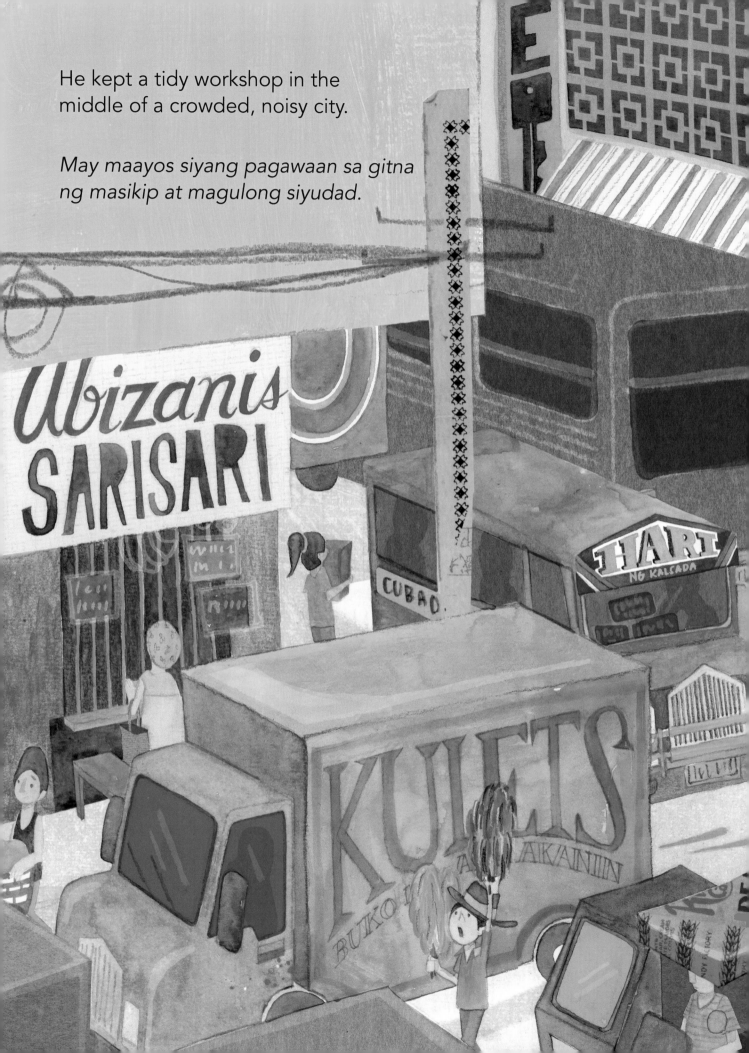

One day the mayor stormed
into Mang Andoy's workshop.

*Isang araw,
sinugod ng alkalde
ang pagawaan ni
Mang Andoy.*

"It's chaos out there!
Nobody's following the rules!"

His big feet stamped on the wooden floor.
His hands cut the air around him in big loops.

"So Andoy, make some signs!"

DO NOT CROSS THE STREET.

NO LOITERING!

DO NOT CROWD.
GET IN LINE.

NO littering!

"When you have them ready,"
the mayor said,
"put them up
in the right places."

*"Maligalig sa labas!
Sinusuway ang mga patakaran!"*

Nagdabog ang malalaki niyang paa sa sahig na kahoy.
Pabilog-bilog ang kumpas ng kaniyang kamay.

"Kaya Andoy, gumawa ka ng mga karatula!"

HUWAG TUMAWID
SA KALSADA.

BAWAL TUMAMBAY!

HUWAG
MAGSIKSIKAN.
PUMILA.

BAWAL magkalat!

"Kapag nayari na," bilin ng alkalde,
"isabit mo na sa mga tamang lugar."

Mang Andoy took out his pencil,
his rulers, and the yellow paint.

He began to work.
The mayor did not like to wait.

Inihanda ni Mang Andoy ang kaniyang lapis,
ang mga panukat, at ang pinturang dilaw.

Agad siyang nagsimula.
Ayaw ng alkalde nang pinaghihintay.

When Luisa came home after school, she put her things down
and went to see what her grandfather was doing.

She read each sign, and then she took his hand.
"Lolo," she said, "is the Mayor angry with us?"

Nang nakauwi si Luisa mula sa eskuwela,
inilapag ang kaniyang mga gamit at tiningnan ang ginagawa ng lolo.

Binasa niya ang bawat karatula, at pinigil ang kamay ng lolo.
"Lolo," aniya, "galit ba sa atin ang Alkalde?"

Mang Andoy took a second look at his signs.
Luisa was right.
He painted them over and started again.

Muling sinipat ni Mang Andoy ang kaniyang mga karatula.
Tama si Luisa.
Pininturahan niya ang mga ito at muling nagsimula.

He worked a long time.
Luisa fell asleep waiting for him.

Kay tagal niyang lumikha.
Nakatulog si Luisa
sa paghihintay sa lolo.

The next day Mang Andoy put the signs up.

Kinabukasan, ipapaskil na ni Mang Andoy
ang mga karatula.

He put one sign at the street corner.

Ipinako niya ang isang karatula sa kanto.

He put another near
the bus stop.

*Idinikit niya ang isa
malapit sa himpilan ng bus.*

He put another
near some benches…

*Isinabit niya ang isa
malapit sa bangkô…*

and the last one by the big trash can.

*at ipinaskil ang huling karatula
sa may malaking basurahan.*

Then they stayed to watch.

At nanatili sila upang magmasid.

Everyone was happy.

Masaya ang lahat.

Even the mayor.

Maging ang alkalde.

ABOUT THE AUTHOR

MAILIN PATERNO has always been fascinated by stories, and she has always wanted to write for children. Some of her books include *Sampaguita* (Cacho Publishing), *The Girl Who Fell from the Sky* (Tahanan Books), and *Fruit Stall* (Ayala Museum). She won the Salanga Prize given by the Philippine Board on Books for Young People in 1986, and the Palanca Awards for Short Story for Children in 1989 and 1991.

Mailin teaches at The Beacon Academy in Laguna province. She lives in Makati City with her husband, two children, and two dogs.

ABOUT THE ARTIST

ISABEL ROXAS is a whimsical artist with a taste for the slightly odd and uncommon, and for tales that go awry.

She has illustrated numerous children's books in both the United States and her native Philippines. Publication highlights include *A Day at the Market* (Winner, 2010 Philippine National Children's Book Award) and the New York Times best-seller *Goodnight Songs* (a collection of poems by Margaret Wise Brown, published by Sterling Press). Isabel's latest picture book, *The Case of the Missing Donut,* was published by Dial Books for Young Readers.

When she's not commuting to and from Manila, Isabel lives in New York City with her husband. In her free time she likes to visit libraries, post offices, and museums as well as collect imaginary pets.

What the Signs Mean in English:

Pagod ka na? Magpahinga muna — *Tired? Rest here*
Paraanin ang isa't-isa — *Make way for each other*
Itapon ang basura dito — *Throw your garbage here*
Mas ligtas tumawid dito — *It's safer to cross here*
Magbigayan — *Give way to each other*